A Priceless Nest

KRISTIINA EHIN

Translated by Ilmar Lehtpere

OLEANDER PRESS

The Oleander Press Ltd
16 Orchard Street
Cambridge
CB1 1JT
England

ISBN 0906672929
ISBN 9780906672921

A CIP catalogue record for the book is available from the British Library.

Cover illustration by Kristiina Ehin
Typeset by Hamish Symington in 10pt Syntax
Printed and bound in Great Britain

Kristiina Ehin was born in Rapla, Estonia in 1977. She received an M.A. in Comparative and Estonian Folklore from Tartu University in 2004. She has published five volumes of poetry in her native Estonia and has won a number of prizes there, including Estonia's most prestigious poetry prize for a volume written during a year spent as a nature reserve warden on an uninhabited island off Estonia's north coast. She has also published an Estonian-English volume of selected poems, a book of short stories and has written a play as well. *The Drums of Silence* (Oleander, 2007), a volume of her selected poems in English translation, was awarded the Poetry Society Corneliu M. Popescu Prize for European Poetry in Translation in 2007. She is often invited to take part in international arts and literary festivals and her work, poetry and prose, appears regularly in English translation in leading Irish and British literary magazines. A new volume of selected poems in a trilingual Estonian-English-Irish edition is published by Coiscéim. Another new collection of English translations of her poetry is in preparation, to be published by Arc in the UK in 2010. *Päevaseiskaja,* a bilingual Estonian-English book of Estonian fairy tales is published by Huma and a Welsh language edition of *The Drums of Silence* will be published by Barddas.

Ilmar Lehtpere had a bilingual upbringing in Estonian and English. He is the translator of Kristiina Ehin's *The Drums of Silence* (Oleander, 2007), awarded the Poetry Society Popescu Prize for European Poetry in Translation. His other translations of Kristiina Ehin's work are *Põletades pimedust – Burning the Darkness – An Dorchadas á Dhó* (Coiscéim, 2009), *Päevaseiskaja – Estonian Fairy Tales* (Huma, 2009) and *Noorkuuhommik – New Moon Morning* (Huma, 2007). A new collection of Kristiina Ehin's poetry in his translation will be published in the UK by Arc in 2010.

Some of these translations first appeared in the following publications:
'The Spy and the Kitten' in *Orbis*
'Pagans in the Bank' in *Crannóg*
'Hard Times' in *The Stinging Fly*, and in *My Brother Is Going off to War* by Kristiina Ehin and Hella Wuolijoki (Lapwing, 2007)

This translation is published with the support of a Traducta grant from the Cultural Endowment of Estonia.

Contents

Pipe-playing-woman and Bomb-laying-woman

PIPE-PLAYING-WOMAN SAT ON the edge of the bed and examined the soles of her slumbering husband's feet. The man was now in the sixth year of a very deep sleep. The woman had just been reading a book about how to predict the future by the lines on the soles of the feet. *Nothing to rejoice at, I'm afraid*, she thought. Suddenly she noticed a thin furrow that went from the man's right heel straight across his Achilles' tendon to his ankle, where the long hairs started that could just as well have belonged to some wild animal. *Ooh*, the woman thought, *a ray of hope!* She went gaily to the balcony and started to play her pipe. She sat on a green stool, fingered the slender pipe, put the mouthpiece to her lips and caressed its insides with her breath. Outside it was May and the first leaves were everywhere so very green, as if the world had just been created at that moment. The woman played and played and felt how she seemed to grow from the sounds she was creating. She was no longer just a woman sitting here on the balcony; she was up in the air, doing gymnastics on the edge of the balcony, twirling on the roof, gambolling in the park in the distance all at the same time, everywhere the sound of her pipe reached.

The sound of her pipe also reverberated in a garden house slanting over to one side at the edge of the park. There lived a black-haired woman. In the course of her life she had done all sorts of work and travelled to many distant lands. Now she wanted to have the peace and quiet to create something truly unquiet. *So be it*, she thought, opened the veranda window, and filled her glass with hot tea from a three-litre jar. The cherry tree blossoming directly next to the veranda strewed petals through the window into her tea glass. The woman admired the cherry blossoms on the dark surface of her tea and her own lovely nails coming into blossom, took a deep breath and in her thoughts thanked the piper. *How good it is of her to play today!* It was a full moon Wednesday, which the woman had been waiting for for a long time. Today she wanted to try out a recipe she had found in the cellar of an old time-worn house. She knew what she was going to make from it – bombs. *First of all the heart of a cuckoo, then a piece of clay with the dried footprint of a frog, then seven ladlefuls of water from the last snowfall…* All of this disappeared into the pot and Bomb-making-woman bent over to stir contentedly. Then the rust of an old axe, the stems of six young nettles and six bags of that reddish powder, fine as dust, that she had found in the very same cellar. Good. The woman stirred. The flame blazed on the cooker and the woman's cheeks and lips turned phlox-purple from the heat and the never-before-known smell. And finally, the whiskers of a white male cat. She had almost forgotten that. She pushed the pot off the flame, put a green shawl with roses round her shoulders, and hurried out with high hopes.

Pipe-playing-woman was just resting, propping her head up on her hands as she looked out onto the street. She saw the black-haired woman with the phlox-purple lips luring cats that, however, all fled from her at the last moment.

What are you looking for? Pipe-playing-woman called.

The whiskers of a white male cat, answered the black-haired woman self-assuredly.

I'll bring you some, we have a white tom, called Pipe-playing-woman.

She went back into the room, picked up the scissors, walked with a decisive air past the cat straight to her sleeping husband, lifted his trouser leg, and cut ten hairs off his right ankle. As she handed them down from the balcony, the women's fingers touched and they looked genially into each other's light eyes.

You play beautifully, play some more, the black-haired woman said and hurried back to the heat of her cooker.

Pipe-playing-woman played all evening. Lanterns lit up in the gardens, moths fluttered around in the light springtime air. The black-haired woman sat at her veranda table and rolled the cool but still strangely glowing dough into bombs. Finally. The woman felt how wonderful it was to be alive when your life has a purpose, and the achievement of this is so close that you have only a few hours to wait – for the slow rising of the full moon over the springtime outskirts of the city. Then the woman started dropping off the bombs. From her green rosy shawl she dropped the dark little cakes under bushes and in staircases and threw them quietly onto balconies. *Plop*, a soft bomb fell on the balcony where Pipe-playing-woman had just been playing.

The black-haired woman flushed with excitement; she had hidden the last bomb against her own breast. The moon had risen over the roofs. And if anyone had heard the strong, rapid drumming of her heart, they might very well have taken fright. The woman felt she was full of a great and secret power, and that she was waiting together with every bomb in the darkness of the bushes, the peace of the balconies, the silence of the staircases and yards.

Far away in the distance a door slammed, a sudden gust of wind passed through the park into the garden and a mass of cherry blossoms settled onto the table. Pipe-playing-woman's chalk-white tom jumped in through Bomb-laying-woman's veranda window and, purring, settled himself down on the cherry blossoms that had been scattered onto the table. By the light of the moon and the cherry blossoms the black-haired woman saw that all of the tomcat's whiskers were in their place.

At that very same moment Pipe-playing-woman's husband, who had hoped to sleep until he died without knowing the purpose of life, woke up. Next to him he felt the woman moist with spring, who was so happy that her husband had woken up that she didn't dare to move. What a beautiful night! The man kissed and kissed the woman ever more and more urgently. Now the woman only wanted to be here, here... The clock struck its last ringing peals... Here!

A slow explosion started that someone had been planning since the beginning of time. Powerfully, unceasingly, it lasted a long, long time, and no one remained as they had been before. *Did you hear me playing my pipe through your sleep?* Pipe-playing-woman asked her husband. *Surely*, the man answered, and suddenly felt he had slept off all his weariness of life.

The white tomcat dozed purring on the cherry blossoms and the black-haired Bomb-laying-woman along with him. The last bomb against her breast had blown itself out of existence, and the woman dreamt that she had set in motion a water mill wheel bursting into blossom. Slowly, creaking, it was pushed ever faster by the river and the white blossoms fell into the black timeless flow. Upon waking in the morning she just knew that she was a born bomb layer – just as some people were born pipe players... But when Pipe-playing-woman rose in the morning, her husband had already got up, made breakfast for her and given milk to the cat. *What a miracle!* Pipe-playing-woman whispered, and thought with gratitude about the woman with the phlox-purple lips.

Life in the town carried on. There were new bombs and new pipe tunes for those who knew how to listen. There was the creaking of the watermill of time, and the fiery tracks of new as well as age-old kisses.

Fire and Water

I

SUCCULENT DARK GREEN house plants in the small bedroom stretched out. The curtains moved in the delicate breeze. Water felt it was hot. She was lying as she had been created, in Fire's arms. Fire felt how Water cooled him yet wasn't able to extinguish him; he felt something very thirsty within him find a sup of refreshment. But with every sup a little part of him died.

Water, said Fire, *do you know what I treasure most in a woman?* Water shook her shoulders and smiled. To tell the truth she had forgotten what woman means. She only felt a warm agitation on her surface, she wanted to move, sway, ripple and lap, and for a long time she felt how much she still had to learn. *I don't know*, she said, *what then?*

I think, said Fire seriously, *the most important thing for a woman is to be naturally bashful.*

Naturally bashful, naturally... what? Water tried to

think but she had forgotten where her head is. She tried to taste what she'd just heard with her tongue. Maybe it was poisonous. Deep within her Water suddenly felt a whirlpool arise, a dark, bottomless centrifuge that tore her away from Fire's arms. Fire flared again with a lighter flame, Water cooled a bit and managed to think a bit more clearly.

Fire eyed Water, who was only just collecting herself and settling down again from the effects of the whirlpool. *You probably aren't... naturally bashful*, he said and cast a few sparks onto Water's still frizzling surface. Water swallowed and caught the sparks in silence.

Water looked inside herself. She was used to cooling and warming. She felt that she lived with every drop and wasn't even afraid of drying up, for whatever dried on land turned into water vapour and soon rained down again from the sky. She was used to going where she could – sometimes as a narrow little rill, other times as a raging river down rapids to a big whirling waterfall, to fall... fall, casting off her own heaviness and clarity, to thrash about and roar and then... in a totally different form somewhere up high to flow on quietly, very quietly. What does bashful mean, what does natural mean, what does woman mean? Water didn't know the answers to those questions and wondered to herself if Fire had ever understood her free-flowing nature at all.

What's wrong? asked Fire. *Come back, I've already become too hot!*

Water drew even further away.

Fire stretched out towards Water and felt that she was cold and obviously so sad that she didn't even sizzle. He tried a different tack – *But for all that you're daring,* he said, *and I like that very much. I like the way you attack me.*

Water smiled a little and lifted her eyes. *Who's bashful, who's natural, who's a woman?,* she asked, and looked into Fire's blood-red heart.

Whoever still knows how to blush, Fire answered without giving his answer too much thought, and saw with a start how Water's grey-blue eyes filled with tears. *There's nothing red in me*, Water thought to herself, utterly downcast, and became very still and clear, like those who are faced with great pain that will not ease. *Look!* whispered Fire, *You're blushing!*

Fire's flame reflected against Water's clear cheeks. And those two restless primal elements lying next to each other did not dare to move, for they were afraid of losing at once that uplifting agitation that is only imparted to those who are very clear.

II

Then the redness faded. Water breathed deeply and understood that it had only been a beautiful moment. The beauty of that moment was only spoilt by the fear that for Fire it may have been too beautiful and too important.

To be able to love you I have to know who I am, said

Water. *If I deceive myself with the thought that there's red in me, that I can blush, then…*

Suddenly Fire understood. He caressed Water and Water had to call up all her strength to withstand Fire's powerful grip.

I love my own red in you, you're the only one I see it in. I only see it because you're Water, the only one strong enough to endure me. You are the only one who is what I am not. Your natural strength is more interesting than bashfulness, more interesting than woman.

The scent of dry unmown grass drifted into the room they were lying in. Normally Fire wanted to set this alight immediately. This time he waited. Outside a bashful drizzle of misty rain started which quickly turned into a huge downpour.

Hard Times

Outside it had been dark as dark can be for several months now. The woman felt like a greenhouse plant that is still alive only thanks to powerful daylight lamps. She felt that she wouldn't be able to deceive herself in this city much longer. Soon she would need something that was real. And she would need a lot of it.

On coming home in the evening the man took his shoes off, and treading softly went to the bedroom and switched the computer on. The computer game, the same one again. Peering over his shoulder at the monitor, the woman saw simplistic tanks, planes and explosions on a big green battlefield. She also saw a white horse.

A white horse... she exclaimed. *Who rides it? You?*

In answer the screen was lit up again by a flaming explosion and the white horse was thrown up in the air. *No, that was some outmoded enemy's horse*, the man explained.

Who are you then? asked the woman.

The Americans, answered the man.

All of them? asked the woman.

The American army.

And who are you conquering?

The Solomon Islands, muttered the man.

The woman thought about the people armies are made up of. The ones who ride white horses, sit in tanks or at computers. She thought of the men of today who after work don't go home when they step through their front door, but to war. They take their shoes off, change their socks and open the computer. To shoot, defeat their enemies, and conquer. To take possession of the Solomon Islands, whatever that might mean. To be everything, for the moment. To be the power. *Well, and why not in hard times like these*, she thought, trying to justify her husband.

The woman sat on the bed and started to massage the soles of her feet. They hurt, especially somewhere in the middle, between the heel and the ball of the foot. It was gone nine o'clock. She lay down with her head on the pillow and rested, closed her eyes and opened them again. She saw the man's broad back, heard the sound of firing, and imagined how, with every movement of the man's fingers a white horse died in the Solomon Islands – the only being she had liked in this game.

Surely a person has to be able to live out his fantasies, surely this game releases energy that grown-up, civilized men can't use up in the course of the day, she thought, trying to understand. But even in that light she didn't like the fact that when the man came home he was really going to war and she had to stay behind and wait for him. She didn't like the fact that he killed, be it only in a computer game, a virtual world, but nevertheless here in their home. Really. It wasn't the something real the woman was craving. Times were hard but, after all, perhaps not as hard as they used to be. She undid her plaits and combed her long hair for a long time. *Men used to really go to war – for ten or even twenty-five years,* she thought, *to die or come home again – crippled and grey-haired, with a few kopecks in their pockets. To come home when their mothers were already dead, and their sisters and beloveds had grown old. The women hardly knew the old cripple who hobbled up to their gate one evening. They helped the man, or more precisely what was left of the man, from his horse, and washed the war off him before they allowed him into the house, the place so long yearned for. And the first thing they asked was, did he often think of them when he was away at war? And did he desperately want to come home? "I wanted a better sword, a miraculous healer and an armoured immortal horse," the man mumbled. And the women shrank back, unable to understand the coldness of this answer from the man only just returned from war. The answer that draws a remorseless line between men and women, sisters and brothers, mothers and sons.*

It is the very same line that the woman now does not know how to cross in this dusky bedroom. She looks at the man's broad back and feels how little this back is together with her. Or perhaps nevertheless... *Isn't it good in some way to be behind this back, opposite the screen, and not to watch the fiery death of white horses and... Isn't it a reason to be happy, that the front line doesn't go through her, but two metres away between the man and the computer. Isn't it good to know that even if the Solomon Islands' gory battlefield begins two metres away, she is lying here on her grandmother's rosy blanket. And even though the man has been away at war for an unbearably long time – so long that she has started to sigh and wring her hands – there is still hope that he won't come back after decades as a cripple, but this evening, perhaps just a little bit blinder and more stooped from sitting at the computer.*

And finally he does come, with no idea of what she has been thinking and feeling during his absence, what game she has been playing behind his back in her imagination – so far and yet so close to the perils of the front line. He switches off the computer and the lamp, and lies down on the bed next to the woman to rest a bit after the gruelling battle. She is already fast asleep, for otherwise she would murmur the questions left on her lips before drifting off – *Did you think of me when you were away at war? Did you desperately want to come home?*

A Priceless Nest

I

A WOMAN WAS lying in a dark room and felt rather than saw how an old black-barked pear tree was strewing delicately light blossoms outside the window. *As if someone was grating moonlight,* she thought, and a pleasant tremor passed through her breast. Suddenly a nightingale started singing on the pear tree so beautifully that the woman felt how a black, sweet feeling of love awoke again in her heart. Angrily she arrayed herself in the dark. A chain of pale snail shells round her neck. Tangerine-coloured bracelets round her wrists, opaque beads in her ears, and over all this ringing lustre a soft shawl, which helped her move without being heard. Barefoot she stepped onto the lawn and the cold dew somewhat cooled her fiery feelings.

I just simply can't... mumbled the woman. Her breast was throbbing so very hard, the pear tree scattering its fragrance so very madly, the nightingale chirruping far too beautifully. The woman stepped closer, stretched herself out and with her heated hand picked the brown bird off the branch. The woman's touch was so delicate and the nightingale was so deep in the spell of its own song that it didn't notice anything. With the other hand the woman grasped her left breast firmly and opened it like the cover of a secret drawer. Under her breast there was an empty space and this space was framed by strong cage walls. The woman put the nightingale into the cage and closed the breast door. Click. *A couple of hundred silver marks, more or less,* the woman thought and knew that now she could nod off in peace. Her heart was light again and free.

The woman slept till dawn brightened, then washed in the amber garden bath, put her hair up adorned with silver flowers, put on her greenish-blue viper-patterned dress, picked up her little black bog-pearl case and stepped through the gate. The sun had already heated up the cobblestones when she got to town. Grey wooden houses lined the streets. A river flowed straight from the sea through the town and into another sea. The river carried foam-white branches and masts broken off ships in a gale, sea badgers and ocean foxes burrowed into the clay banks and a raft drifted up and down the river drawn by a whale. So it had always been, beginning in the mists of time. And beginning in the mists of time women who didn't want to fall in love yet had come to this town to sell whatever it was that threatened to make them feel.

The woman stepped into the pub. She walked through the room and went behind the bar, opened the door and sat down on the snail sofa in the little room.

Very well, we'll take it, said the Blind Man, who was sitting opposite her in a birch chair, when the woman had taken the nightingale out of the cage in her breast and imprisoned it in a small iron cage on the table between them.

The bird chirruped in a voice trembling with pain and its little beak snatched at the rays of sunlight that fell directly on the table from the only window in the room. *It sings well, a good bargain, I found it yesterday evening on a black pear tree,* the woman said with feigned indifference. The Blind Man piled the silver coins directly into the black case and the woman hurried away, not daring to admit to herself how the little bird's song had again filled her heart with mute longing.

From a tradesman she bought small, peculiar, transparent secret eyes and someone's curved ears that had a thin transparent surface like the leaf of a tree. When the woman went to bed that evening, she put the secret eyes in her ears and covered her closed eyes with the thin curved ears. The woman had a man who lay next to her like a hewn log. Like a hewn log this man rolled over onto her every night and the woman dutifully put up with rough touchings that fortunately were too robust to make her feel anything. This time however the man wanted to say something to the woman. His heart was full to the brim with feelings for his own dear wife, and he had been thinking for a long time how he could show her. He correctly sensed that he had still not managed to touch the land behind her eardrums, along which the road to her heart might lead. But the woman saw him through her secret eyes, bought with the money from the sale of the nightingale and now stuffed in her ears, and listened to him with the ears that had once belonged to who knows who and now tightly covered her beautiful eyes. No wonder then that nothing in the woman moved when the man once again rolled onto her like a dense, heavy tree trunk and whispered, breathing heavily in her ear, *I'm so in love with you, oh you're so ferociously beautiful, I'm waiting for you to grow older so I can marvel at you in peace without my eyes starting to hurt.*

The woman didn't hear him, she only saw the man's mouth and teeth with the aid of the secret eyes stuffed into her ears, at the same time as her keen new curved ears picked up a never before heard rustling in the room. With a deep sigh the tree trunk rolled off the woman and fell asleep with his mouth open like a tree hollow.

The woman quickly removed her secret eyes and ears, dropped them on the floor next to the bed and listened again. There was no doubt about it – there was a snake in the room. It had slithered in through the window by the light of the moon. Now it undulated across the floor, with a quick movement snapped up the woman's secret eyes and ears with its forked tongue and swallowed them down.

Then it climbed up into the bed, wound its way onto the man's chest and slipped into the hollow of his mouth. *Common marsh adder, doesn't bother me,* the woman thought, and fell asleep.

The next morning her husband was like a new man. His eyes sparkled light green and a strange feeling came over the woman. *Your presence is making me feel strange, go somewhere else,* she said, putting on her normal tone of voice.

But the man said nothing and just looked at her with a smile.

The woman went outside and started washing herself. But as soon as she touched the water in the amber bath it started boiling. She scalded her fingers and angrily went back inside. The man looked at her again, pulled the woman towards him and said, *Wonderful.*

What's wonderful? the woman asked, but the man didn't answer. He kissed her fervently and long, like never before. The adder slithered boldly from the man's mouth in between the woman's lips and filled, quivering, her throat and oesophagus. The snake looked for a moment into the woman's stomach and backed quickly into the man again. The woman would have clawed the man but the tips of her fingers hurt and so instead she raised them high in the air. She pushed him away from her with her breast, quickly opened the door of her left breast with her teeth and leapt on the man so that he disappeared entirely into the cage of her heart. Click. The door of her breast closed.

I've brought you a log the size of a man, inside of which there is an adder, inside of which in turn there is... the woman said breathlessly, for this time she had come to town running. Quickly-quickly she wanted to sell what filled her heart and made it so heavy. She hadn't managed to open the door of her breast yet when the Blind Man answered, *This deal is no deal. I'm not buying this.* The woman was dismayed and took her leave. Her hands were throbbing with pain and she pressed them to her breast. *Adder, fie,* she whispered, and smiled unwillingly.

II

Come on, explain! The woman was breathing heavily, and nearly screamed at the man. She had opened the door of her breast and the man had climbed out onto the fluffy bedspread, which was covered with a greyish evening light.

Wait, just let me orient myself, the man answered. He rose from the bed and stretched. He clicked his teeth together once, stepped out across the veranda into the yard, smelled the pear tree blossoms, smelled them again, ran around the house a few times, stepped onto the steps, thought again and ran off across the meadow, yellow with cowslips, into the forest.

There's a forest path knotted with tree roots that way full of hollows. Maybe he's taking his adder back, the woman thought. She lay down on the bedspread and was just beginning to feel like herself again when the man returned.

And? Did you get rid of that creature? the woman asked, astir with expectation.

What creature? The woman didn't know what to answer. She got angry again, tied the man up and hoisted him up by the feet to hang from the ceiling.

Open your mouth, she commanded. The man thought he might as well just for the fun of it, and spread his jaws out wide. The woman had poured good whole milk into a bowl and put it invitingly on the floor. But the adder didn't appear. She drank the milk herself, untied the man, went outside and sighed heavily.

Maybe she'd got the feeling wrong? Maybe the snake was still inside her? Maybe it hadn't gone back into the man? It just could be... Her heart skipped a few beats, she filled her lungs with the velvet evening air and didn't notice how a swarm of nightingales had gathered on the black pear tree, all of them chirruping clearly and mercilessly about the beauty, the pain and the loss of freedom that grips lovers.

The adder stayed on to live in the woman and the man, filling them with secrets the cage in the woman's heart was incapable of holding and no milk was sweet enough to tempt out. It came and went as it pleased, it wandered unperturbed out of one and into the other. The woman didn't know how to explain the feelings that surged within her, but it seemed easier to make them her own than to struggle against them. She hoped and feared, loved and suffered until she seemed to turn into a log herself – a strong, knobbly sculpture of love, a priceless nest. The best one the adder had ever known.

Festival of Joy

"For his mercy is on those who fear him," the pastor finished his reading. The congregation sang "aaaamenn, aaaameeeenn" and sat down amid the creaking of the wooden pews. I slipped in with my mother. It was holy Christmas Eve and we were late. As always.

This time there wasn't even a lack of places to sit in the church, we found seats in a side recess. It was cold. I pulled my coat together over my knees. Rosy-cheeked old ladies, some alone, some still next to grey-haired old gents, sat on the bluish pews, hands modestly in their laps, eyes on the song sheets. "Issand on siin, lõppegu häda ja piin – the Lord is here, an end to trouble and pain," the ladies sang in their high-pitched voices and the men were hoarsely and seriously silent. The odd one here and there did open his mouth but closed it again quickly, for even most of the women couldn't reach such a high pitch.

A German priest once visited Estonia and Livonia in the

grey times and later wrote that Estonians do indeed love to sing, but each in their own particular voice, loud and with all their heart. All together it was reminiscent of a bleating herd of sheep. Now it was reminiscent of a choir of angels whose song had broken off out of great piety and humility.

The next song was "üks roosike on tõusnud – a rose has sprouted up" and singing along I tried to find my voice, tried to think of the heartening, stalwart God of my childhood, who for some reason was the image of my grandfather, a God who didn't suffer from an inferiority complex, and who didn't need to be feared in order to show mercy. I looked towards the altar and found that of all the pious figures of little old men my God most resembled Saint Christopher, who stood straddling over the altar. This man in red garb, with the outward appearance of Hercules, was said to have once carried the little Christ over a river.

I tried to sing in a joyful, natural voice, like on some sunny summer morning while making coffee, like at some happy moment in my life when I had felt close to God. A man standing in front of me turned round and looked at me in bewilderment. He had probably never heard such a joyful voice in church before, and he probably couldn't decide if he liked it or not. I fell silent.

"Behold, I bring you good tidings of great joy: for unto you is born this day in Bethlehem a Saviour," thundered the pastor, but no one in the church seemed to be joyful. And already following the lead of the organ the old ladies were singing the next little song: "See on see ilus lapsuke, kes meie rõõm ja kallis õnn – it is that lovely little child, our joy and dearest blessing." I had given up...

The organ boomed, the wind outside howled. I thought of the crows I had seen cowering on the churchyard wall. I thought of my hundreds of ancestors who had cowered in church like freezing crows, bent over in fear, clearly not understanding this joy and unable to imagine how someone in the distant town of Bethlehem could be born as our Saviour and pour blessings into our cold bones. But they probably believed more than me – hell and sin, piety and virtue. I thought of the women who for centuries had again and again given birth to fill these church pews. They did this in dark smoke saunas, behind a hayrick alongside work, on soft moss in the forest, in more wretched conditions than Mary. I thought of the women who hadn't been granted the precious blessing to believe that their child was the Redeemer, the Saviour, the Messiah; who – in contrast to Mary – because of that very same Annunciation had begun to believe that their child was the fruit of sin, and girls already at birth more sinful than boys. No worshipping shepherds, not a single king, no frankincense or myrrh...

"Neil karjastel väljal küll mures on meel, sest patuste lootus ei ilmu ju veel. Mis Aabrami kinnitus, Iisaku rõõm, Mis Jaakobi julgus ja Taaveti kroon, ja Taaveti kroon – the shepherds in the field are troubled, for the hope of sinners has still not appeared. Abraham's avowal, Isaac's joy, Jacob's courage and David's crown, and David's crown..." At the last Taavet, or David, the voice had to be torn so high that only an elderly singing teacher in a black beret managed to sing it. She looked round and stood up in a punctilious fashion. We sinners stood up after her to hear the next part of the Word of God.

I remembered how my grandfather had taught me that song once long ago. The wind howled outside the same as today and the idiotic prohibitions of Soviet times filled my heart with the sweet joy of Christmas.

Then my grandfather taught me "Oh Christmas Tree" and then two patriotic songs, and finally "Silent Night," which in Estonian ends "Sleep, joy of sinners – sleep, joy of sinners". I repeated this, mumbling, and fell asleep in the armchair in his room, not understanding who was a sinner or why joy had to sleep.

Now in this modern church the wish arose in me to slip out. I felt that most of the people here were like me. They had come more out of some feeling of nostalgia than belief. My mother wanted to leave too. *Let's stop on the way, let's not just storm out.*

We stopped then a few times as we made our short way, lifting our eyes reverently to the altar like born hypocrites. Quietly we opened the creaking door and slid out into the winter night, which was cold and bitingly honest.

Pagans at the Bank

I WANTED TO make a money transfer, but it turned out that not a single machine for the movement of money in the centre of Tartu was working. I was even given to understand in three languages by the last machine in the lobby of a tall bank building that it was out of order. The bank workers were bustling around it like vergers around a priest who had fainted in the middle of his sermon. People were standing in the queue, all of them holding bankcards between their fingers like prayer books. But the priest just didn't want to come round. The bank workers-vergers had no time for even a word to their congregation and most of the people in the queue went away swearing. I observed with interest how this machine is able to faint in such a young-lady-of-the-manor way. Must be tired, I thought, startled that I could attribute such human feelings to this lump of cables, iron and glass.

I stepped in beneath the high arches of the bank. In front of me there was a countryman, cap in hand, who didn't know which button to press to get a number for his turn, or confession. I explained that the first button is the safest.

We stood meekly against the wall like a father and daughter and looked up at the brightly flashing numbers, which were very reminiscent of hymnal numbers on the wall of of a church. *Don't even dare to start daydreaming here, or your number might slip by without you noticing,* the old man mumbled. But I started watching the clouds anyway, which by some miracle were glowing through the darkly opalescent stained glass window of the bank. I gave a sudden start, as if waking from a dream, when my number came up.

What sins have you committed, my child? I heard the cashier, who was much the same age as me, ask.

None, I heard myself answer.

But why have you come, my child? One comes here with one's troubles.

Oh, yes, I heard myself answer again, fingering the pearl pattern stitched onto my purse as if it were a rosary, *I don't know how to make a money transfer if the machines for that purpose are out of order.*

Very well, my child, give me the money.

I handed the money over. *And then three kroon service charge, as you must be over twenty-five, and then twelve kroon for the transfer.*

I looked nervously for cent and one kroon coins. *Ah, I've got it!*

So, to the poor belongs the Kingdom of Heaven. Who would you like to send the money to?

I gave the person's name and account number.

So, excellent, he is also a member of our bank's congregation. What would you like to put as the purpose?

I'd heard somewhere, perhaps in a dream, that it's safest to say a debt.

It's a debt. I cast my eyes down discreetly.

Ah, so that's how things stand, peace be with you my child, in twenty minutes he will receive your money.

My friend who I was sending the money to was, suitably, in America. I imagined how the winged bank horses would gallop over the ocean, their golden horseshoes flashing, my banknotes in a golden bag around their necks, how they would foam, and stop to rest in Greenland, then kick out and storm on.

My daydreams were interrupted by the cashier's voice, which had suddenly become insistent: *And have you become a member of our cumulative pension scheme?*

I strained my brain but had no idea what she was on about, although I seemed to have heard somewhere that this was a good thing. But the cashier's voice frightened me. She almost screamed at me: *At the moment it's FREE OF CHARGE!!! Do it without fail! Do it now! Sign here. Ah, you don't know, my child? What is there to know, it takes just a second and it's done. Of course we can't force you, but give us your signature anyway. Ah, you have no time now? How is that?*

I backed away in alarm. The cashier's black-fingernailed hands stretched out towards me holding a sheet of paper and a pen, and her beautifully painted eyes looked at me full of sympathy, as if I were an idiot who had turned down a free lunch.

Give us your signature! she called once more.

Give us three drops of blood! I heard, and closed the door, bumping into the shy countryman, and we walked together towards the main door with our fingers securely at the bottom of our empty pockets.

Good-bye, God bless!

God bless!

Cumulative pension scheme? What is to be gained from that by anyone – as young as me? As old as him? As poor as the both of us?

A Silent Man

I

THE NATIONAL ANTHEM is already sounding all the way from Toompea. Through frost-covered Tallinn the melody carries quite a distance as it accompanies the setting sun. The woman straightens a rug with her foot, sweeps up bread crumbs off the floor, organizes the things she had thrown about in a burst of anger yesterday. Everything had started again with the man's silence, his being so unshakably wordless, for which the woman could find no reason. This angered her, put her on edge, made her say things she now regretted…

How strange the way I change, she muses. *I had only just thought that I would never make up. That I would use the last of my money for a ticket to Brazil, Lübeck, Greenland or the Crimea. To simply flee as a protest, unable to really change anything. That I would take the laptop and sit in a restaurant and write all day, turn the telephone off, defiantly go for walks along the seaside... and now... it all seems simply childish.*

The woman takes a deep breath and thinks about the conversation they had only arrived at that morning, when all her tears had flowed until there wasn't a drop left, when she had stormed at the man in a fit of rage, beat her fists until they hurt, attacked him like a lynx, all the while understanding that with every burst of anger, every belligerent question asking why, every reproachful attempt at explanation, she distanced herself from the man even more. Finally, worn out, dispirited by her own broken spirit, she fell asleep, her hand holding the nape of his neck, which was turned towards her.

You're like a mountain, she whispered, *an armoured mountain. Or no, more like a turtle! You draw yourself into your shell and wait for the storm to pass.* Suddenly through her burning anger she felt great tenderness, tenderness for this shell wearer who was so tender inside, and this gave her the strength to fall asleep.

I have a feeling that you've been pretending for two days now, the man had said in the morning as they sat like two injured birds on the edge of their nest and, bit by bit getting over the fear of demeaning themselves, started talking to each other again. The woman understood that this was the sort of honesty the man expressed still from the safety of his shell. She understood that any sort of sharp reply would make him close up within himself, falling silent in self-protection. The woman endured a pause.

The man continued: *Yesterday I wanted to get out of this game, to be far away. I instilled myself with the belief that it doesn't touch me.*

The woman breathed in to stop the pain from burning. She stretched her back, shifted herself to sit more comfortably and breathed out with a murmur. *Did you think you wanted to be out of our game altogether, and where we've arrived at for the time being, or just yesterday evening's... game?* She asked boldly, very much fearing that he would answer, *Both.*

No, only yesterday evening's, the man answered, after taking time to think about it. The woman breathed again in relief. The fury in her cooled a little. It was no longer so difficult to talk reasonably.

In what sense am I pretending? she asked. The man didn't answer for a long time and the woman didn't understand what he was thinking. She tried to think along and asked, *Do you think that tears are too cinematic, that they're a way of earning sympathy and caring? That they're some dishonest dodge allowed to women?*

The man coughed, and a slight sense of dread came over the woman from that cough. *I think*, said the man, *that you have to come to terms with your feelings by yourself. That your moods are not my fault. If I help you once you'll begin to depend on that.*

You're wrong, the woman raised her voice, knowing

that she was breaking her promise to speak calmly. *I don't manipulate and I don't pretend, I really was sad. That's why I cried. It wasn't your fault. But when you said nothing, nothing and nothing and didn't notice my pain, then my sadness turned to anger that you were the cause of. And your silence blew my anger ablaze until in the end I was engulfed in flames.*

The man said nothing, grimly, and the woman forced herself to be calm again. *I wasn't pretending, I really was sad*, she repeated quietly.

It was a grey mid-morning. Through the window it could be seen that the air was very cold.

It's getting hot. I have to go to work now, the man said and got up.

Wait, how far did we get? the woman asked. She wanted the fact that they had talked, shared their thoughts instead of rage or silence, to have some outcome. She wanted to arrive at a way of doing things differently another time.

But the man went in order to come back soon, and they stretched their little fingers to each other in parting, exchanged timorous glances that no longer had a shell between them.

It's got better after all, the woman thought and went for a walk in the park. In the light of the bright daylight lanterns the fat ducks crept along on the frozen pond, the tree trunks were mid-winter mottled, the moss on them somehow especially bright green. For several weeks everything had dripped, splashed and gurgled. Now it was quieter and every slightest sound in the frozen world echoed, barely audible. *The only possibility, my only possibility is to learn the language of silence, learn to read the words behind a closed mouth, feelings that may be too raw to be expressed, and thoughts that, on becoming words, might finish building us, like a town. And then the flood would come. And that would be an answer too, only we wouldn't hear it anymore,* the woman thought.

The sun had set long ago, the anthem had hummed an end to the day. The woman's footsteps echoed clearly on the half frozen pavement.

II

That evening everything started just like the time before. The woman wasn't able to bear the man's silence and went instead into the other room. She sat in the armchair at the writing table and pulled her knees up under her chin. This foetal position always gave her strength, and this time it did too. Thoughts and feelings started to slowly take on some coherent form. She started writing, the sentences came short and told more of what happened than of what was thought and felt. The words were rough and certain.

In between she made tea – a mix of strong herbs and black tea, wrapped her fingers round the big warm cup, drank, wrote and drank, looked out of the window at how the winter evening glowed everywhere – in the air, on the two church steeples in the distance, the framework of a crane, the roof of a neighbouring house, every frozen, leafless branch.

Now she wrote about her dreams, those scarce, shy beings who bent over her in the night to drink from the river of her consciousness, and whose reflections she was accustomed to keeping in her memory. The words became gentler, the sentences longer and more supple. The activity was no longer as important as the feeling or state of mind that had to be carefully painted. She had to choose her words, even create new ones. Calling dreams to mind is a state that completely enfolds a person deep into themselves. Touch, sound, smell – everything is important but, above all, watchful tranquillity and the ability to wait for new dream pictures to come to mind. And now she did remember a dream from yesterday. Hastily she thought it through to the end. She had all the different parts she assured herself, and quickly started writing. It was a special dream – a reality that common consciousness can't think up, a coloured pearl in her collection of dreams, full of illogical logic that in some peculiar fashion shook everything into place.

Night had fallen. The woman smiled to herself and put her pen down. Taking her teacup to the kitchen, she met the man. He again didn't say anything. Like a big warm animal he went his ways, and for some reason the woman felt she had to hide her joy from him.

III

The man still kept his silence the next day and the day after that, and the woman ran out of things she wanted to do by herself.

Does he think about us the way I do? Is he suffering? Is he trying to find clarity, the strength to carry on? Or is he taking revenge? But what for? These questions droned constantly in her mind.

One evening when the man came home once again after her, the woman didn't rush to the door to meet him. She lay on the bed under a thin blanket, sipped tea from a big blue earthenware mug and said nothing. She just didn't feel like doing anything. And looking at the man simply made her feel like getting sick.

She wasn't offended, but she was disappointed and sad. And to tell the truth she felt it didn't matter if there was anyone with her in this flat or not. Her love and caring had suddenly been replaced by great indifference.

Hours and hours went by and meanwhile the man asked her something. Over a period of a week he passed a few words over to the other edge of the abyss. Only now they bounced straight back off the woman's eardrums. And beyond an unintelligible grunt the man got no answer.

The woman was reminded that when they had only just met, and were sitting in garden chairs, drinking lemonade and looking at the evening sky, the man had said, *I think talking spoils love. Words put cracks in feeling until it crumbles in the end like a plaster figure.* And she – was it really her? – had thought, and nodded and said, *Yes, that may well be.*

Now – if she only had the wish to speak – she would answer hotly, *It isn't so, don't be soft in the head! If you don't talk, feelings get no oxygen and they suffocate or become mad like someone locked into a windowless room. Words are windows, fresh air streams through them!*

Now the man came into the room and again went his way like a big warm animal. He sat at the computer, a sauna towel round his hips, and when the woman stole a glance at him from the corner of her eye, that broad-shouldered figure reminded her very much of some ancient god. Who? No, not Zeus or Hermes. Osiris? Perhaps.

Only this silence… Barren as a field in a drought, everything beautiful dying of thirst. *Only words would water this field*, the woman thought, but she had to keep her own words like the very last drops of dew.

The Man with a Passport

THERE ONCE WAS a man who lived with his Passport. They lived together in the same flat. And just across the hall that smelled of cats there lived another man. He didn't live alone either, but rather together with his Driving Papers. Every day the Driving Papers warranted him beautiful dreams. They were so close, they sat in his lap, one more charming than the next. One tickled him under the chin, another caressed him ardently, the third made dinner.

Aren't there a lot of them, aren't they beautiful, isn't the man with the Driving Papers lucky, thought the man who himself only had a Passport. A Passport that for the greater part of the day just passed the time, quietly and out of sorts. And if at first it had seemed lovely to the man, new, secure, fragrant and brimming with empty pages free of visas and untouched by stamps marking his own border crossings, the man was now ever more seldom taken by the mood to hold it in his hands and open it.

To tell the truth he had begun to think about getting a new passport, as he knew he would have to do so one day anyway. The picture he now saw on the first page when he opened his Passport, the picture looking back at him from the front of the Passport, hadn't been him for a long time now.

And the Passport felt that the man, citizen such and such who it belonged to, had become distant, irrevocably different. And however the Passport tried, it somehow wasn't able to bring together this man from the past whose picture warmed against its heart, and this chap shuffling around in slippers who grunted, belched, snored, clicked the TV remote control, and rustled the pages of the automobile sections in the newspapers but ever more seldom the Passport's finely patterned pages. The Passport had become surly, it felt that it was being covered slowly and ever so quietly with a layer of dust. It didn't blossom or glow as it had before, and especially in the morning hours it felt utterly unimportant, almost like the leaflets that are stuffed into their letter box every day. But the man grabbed at just those glossy fliers. He collected them outright, especially car adverts, for one day he would buy himself a car and then he too would get…

The neighbour had just come home with his Driving Papers. I wonder if he's ever even had a Passport, the man with the Passport thought. Nowadays a Passport is regarded as much too heavy a book and too uncomfortable to carry around. Maybe one day he could manage with just Driving Papers too? *You might as well take the flag of the republic down off the house*, the Passport grumbled and fell down the side of the armchair. *It's been dark for a long time already, are you the man of the house or not?*

I'm not the only man of the house in this house, the man grumbled quietly, with resignation, and heaved himself up onto his feet. Shrieks of laughter rang out from the neighbouring flat. The man with the Driving Papers must have been splashing around in the jacuzzi he'd installed in his living room. The man with the Passport bit his lip thoughtfully.

II

Two weeks later the man was free of the old Passport that had become so heavy. Now he had a new red-cheeked Passport – as young as the man's heart, which suddenly felt liberated from a heavy load. And what was even more wonderful – the man had an Identity Card, that small, secret and comfortable, magnetic and delicate, influential, easily portable, wallet-decorating plastic card, thin as a fingernail. He hadn't needed to use it yet. But one day, if the red-cheeked clump of a Passport should become the same sort of sullen, passive type like the last one, he'll have the officially sanctioned right to use his Identity Card. The man felt that the Identity Card was as beautiful as the Driving

Papers, which were really a plastic card too. It will probably never age, never wrinkle, tear or burn to ashes.

The neighbours died on one and the same day. They took their last breaths at one and the same moment and heard how their heartbeats became slower and slower until they subsided entirely. The Passport and Identity Card died together with the one, and with the other – his beloved Driving Papers. Before them was a dusty midday road. They stood together next to a yellow car and were just about to cross the border to the other side. The border guard asked for documents. One of them showed his Passport, the other his Driving Papers. The barrier was raised and the way was free, but the car didn't move from the spot.

Where was the accelerator? asked the man with the Driving Papers.

Have you never driven a car before? asked the man with the Passport.

No, I haven't, admitted the man with the Driving Papers, *I bought these papers, I only know how to put caretakers to work.*

But for some reason this car didn't have any caretakers. The Driving Papers and the Identity Card didn't know how to drive either, nor did the man with the Passport. Finally the Passport sat behind the wheel, and before anyone understood what was happening, started the motor and stepped on the accelerator.

A Completely Normal Man

I WOULD NEVER *have believed it... Never believed that something like this could happen to me. To me, her and our unborn child*, the man spelled out more precisely in his thoughts. His wife, his beloved companion in life, had just now left him this very night. She had packed her rucksack, left the keys to the flat on the edge of the bed, and stood in the hall for a long time before leaving. The man had sat huddled on the soft carpet in the bedroom and listened only to the restless, warm pulsing in his stomach.

Have you got anything else to say? the woman had asked from the hall. Her voice was pitiless.

The man didn't answer. This moment just had to be endured. The door from the bedroom to the hall was open and the man felt that his head was completely empty.

Have you got anything to say? the woman asked again abruptly, and the man felt that the woman was actually demanding: *Admit everything, show regret, and perhaps I might be able to stay with you.*

This feeling filled the man with blind rage. It was because of his rage that he was crouching on the carpet, because of his rage that his head was empty, because of his rage that he forced himself to be calm, for he knew that if his and his departing wife's fierce truths collided once more, it would be as total as the collision of two trains. There would be no survivors.

The woman sighed. *Good-bye then*, she said in her old voice and opened the front door. Now life came into the man. He stormed after the woman, who had already turned her back to him and was just about to walk down the stairs of their home for the last time. The man kicked the woman a couple of times in the backside, unleashing his rage for a moment.

Thank you very much for coming by to make a child for me! The man's voice echoed like a bang in the bleak staircase. The woman fled, ignoring his words, down towards the front door. The man closed the door of the flat and without thinking about anything started to clean the kitchen.

When he lay down to sleep the man pressed his hands on his stomach. There was still a warm pulsing and the man felt how exactly in his middle, just in the place that he was most used to regarding as himself, dwelled someone else, new and unknown. This someone was half from himself and half from that woman who just now, in the fourth month of expecting their child, had left him alone.

Solitude. Night – faithful and dark. Night, that always turns its back to you and doesn't tease you for even a moment with thoughts of goodness, understanding, shared responsibility. Now the man was alone in the night. Alone with the child growing in his stomach – the child both of them had wanted.

Is it possible to love a person with no sense of reason? Is it possible to love without considering one's own sense of reason? The man thought it wasn't. That woman certainly had no sense of reason. And the man's reason told him clearly that loving such a person was a waste of resources. But in this dark, faithful, indifferent night the man felt that even if he didn't love that woman anymore, he still loved her hair, every single strand of which was like a strong red snake, hair that was alive and self-contained between his fingers, the scent of which he never tired of breathing in. He felt with his hands for the woman's pillow beside him in the bed and breathed its scent in deeply. More, more... The pillow might only smell of the woman's hair for this one night. Perhaps by tomorrow night the scent on the pillow will have faded forever, as his love for that woman and her hair should soon fade into eternity.

But in his dreams the man saw the woman's eyes. They were warm, radiant and soft as moss. It was impossible to find any cruelty in them. They were honest, resolute eyes, a shade of brown no one else had. Now they changed into small lakes amid a great primeval forest. The man would so have wanted to bend down and drink from them, to moisten his lips in them if only for a moment, yet he still remembered, strangely enough, the promise he made before drifting off: to forget that being without reason, the woman who had betrayed him.

In the morning the man had to rush onto the tram to get to his ultra-sound examination on time. There were other men in the clinic corridor, one of whom, a particularly big-bellied child-bearer, had just came out of the consulting room and now stepped toward the front door with the support of his slender wife. That slender woman held the man gently round the waist, and the delightful giddiness of joy that enveloped them momentarily stabbed the solitary man bitterly in the heart.

It was dark in the consulting room and between the flashing numbers on the screen the man clearly saw the contours of his child. The child had hands, fingers and toes, deep eye sockets, and it moved. It was small and yet unexpectedly big.

Half from me, half from her... Somehow the man couldn't stop thinking about his wife, for the embryonic life wriggling in his middle was hers and now showed itself to the man for the first time. *If my wife were here and saw what I see, she wouldn't be able to even think of leaving.* The man was sure of that.

Kidneys in place, liver in place, spine visible, pulse 152, nuchal translucency 1.4, the doctor dictated to the nurse.

The picture on the wall disappeared. The man got up, dressed, gratefully took the ultra-sound print-outs with him and stepped into the corridor.

I would never have believed... the man thought, and wondered if he had ever before in his life been so overwhelmingly happy and so inconsolably unhappy at the same time.

I'll manage, he assured himself. *I'll manage. I'm strong and healthy, a completely normal man.*

Human Lizard and Cat-Elephant

A MAN AND a woman wake up in the middle of the night at the same time.

Are you sleeping? asks the man.

I don't know, answers the woman, and wonders that her lips are moving. Outside the open window the rain is pattering and the curtains are moving slightly in the cool night breeze. Bit by bit they remember what dreams they have seen, each of them behind their own bright forehead under their closed eyelids. And they both again feel a great wish to sink into a funnel of sleep, and yet to be together, awake for a little. Slowly they remember who they have been until now, and with what thoughts they had fallen asleep yesterday, hoping to sleep peacefully until morning. But the memory of who they have been seems to be a bright star in the blackening night, one of many possibilities.

Then the woman breaks the silence and whispers, *You're a Carcass.*

The man opens his eyes in the dark and hears how the wind slams the window shut. *But you're a Cat,* he says slowly, *a carrion-eating Cat.*

The Cat climbs with its front paws onto the chest of the Carcass and tears at the soft breast meat with its teeth. The thin bones rattle and the Cat whips its tail back and forth to demonstrate, *this prey is mine.*

Nevertheless, says the man calmly, *you're not a real Cat, but rather a small pink Elephant that thinks it's a Cat.* The woman feels that the man is quite on her level tonight.

But you're... a Human Lizard, she whispers. *The top part of you is Human, but the bottom is Lizard.*

The Elephant that thought it was a Cat sprayed water all over the bed from its trunk. That was the only thing that it definitely knew how to do. But the Cat, who loved the dry and the warm, fled into the hall. The Elephant followed it and killed the Cat, removed its skin and cut it into small pieces. From those pieces it made itself a real cat costume. It came back between the wet sheets, but felt it was no longer interesting. *That's what happens when you try to be interesting for someone else's sake,* she thought. *I'll become an animated cartoon, and I really wanted to avoid that.*

I was wrong again, said the man looking at the woman. *You're not simply an Elephant that thinks it's a Cat, you're a Mad Elephant that thinks it's an animated cartoon cat, and at the same time you're a Mad Cat that thinks it was once a real elephant.* Half awake, the woman began to find it a bit interesting between the wet sheets.

The man stroked her slippery wet back and the woman felt how lovely it really was to to be such an Elephant or such a Cat. And being mad was particularly interesting.

She shifted down a bit so that her little pink trunk touched the Lizard's strong slippery head. She smiled under cover of her trunk for she knew that the Human Lizard's identity was nevertheless noticeably stronger than her own at the moment. She only met herself after all those playful and deadly serious years. Still. She whispered, *Lizard Human, Human Lizard...* and looked in turn into the serious penetrating eyes of both the Lizard and the Human.

The only difference between sleeping and waking is you suddenly being aware that I'm awake now, said the Human Lizard in the man's voice. And the woman felt that there was something unusual about him saying that at this moment. Something that prompted forgiveness for words that were left unsaid and therefore deadly in the previous life. And the woman, for whom both the Elephant and the Cat were fighting, knew what she had to do. She said, *Part of you could now be a mirror, as honest a mirror as possible. I want to see myself in you, not all the time, but at least just this once.*

And so it happened. The Human Lizard's stomach became a big mirror with golden edges. The Cat-Elephant slowly lifted her head and looked at herself in it. The Lizard curled itself gently round the woman's slender neck and looked curiously into the mirror.

Well, what do you see? asked the Human.

They saw a city, a city with countless thousands of windows in the evening darkness, thousands of human beings coming from work, thousands of women preparing food, thousands of girls doing themselves up and watching TV before going out. They saw men cowering at work where it seemed they were a little cold. A prodigious force pulled them towards home where their women waited, warm and giving.

The Human Lizard and Cat-Elephant looked at this reflection spellbound. They seemed to drown in it, they didn't see themselves, but they sensed very precisely their own place in that variegated pattern that was too simple to take note of in everyday life, yet always too difficult to keep in mind.

Hah, said the Cat-Elephant. *I'm the one who's cold.* She made her shoulders shiver and breathed the late summer's night air in deeply. *I'm the one who needs warming.* She caressed the Lizard, who had stretched himself out towards her. *You're the one who gives security and warmth. You're the one who waits, the one who gives. I still don't understand anything.*

Nor do I, answered the Human Lizard and they laughed seriously.

The Spy and the Kitten

It was one of those Sundays on which the Spy felt that it was totally impossible to live together with someone, especially with this huge hundred-kilogramme Kitten. She lay in bed and waited for the Kitten to wake up, and thought about a well-known poem. Which is more beautiful – *the love of freedom* or *the freedom of love*? She found that the second was more beautiful and expressive, but that in truth she hadn't reached that level yet.

Do you want coffee? she asked. The Kitten slurped a few mouthfuls from her cup and wanted to sleep on. But the Spy asked, *What would you do if one morning I'd fled and left you a letter on the table: I've gone west to visit my grandmother, to look for the world's most beautiful flower, a plant that cures all illnesses, a country where death holds no sway?*

What would I do? purred the Kitten. *At first I wouldn't even notice the letter for a long time because our table is such a mess.*

Hm, said the Spy. She tried to think of a place in the flat that wasn't such a mess and where the Kitten would discover her letter first thing in the morning. But it was difficult to find such a place. *Doesn't matter. Then I won't leave a letter,* she said. *But at least I've warned you now.*

Warned. The morning was sunny and warm and the Spy already had fresh thoughts in her head. She stretched her slender body again and wanted to jump out of bed, but the Kitten said, *I'd come and find you, I'd tie a cord round your legs and drag you home.*

The Spy gave a start. *How would you find me? I wouldn't take my phone with me.*

I'd put a chip in you and I'd always find you, the Kitten explained.

The Spy didn't know what to say to that.

I'd find the chip inside me and take it out, she said finally.

You wouldn't find it because once I put it in you it would find its own place and crumble into a thousand pieces, each one of which would always show me the way to wherever you are in the universe. You would never find all those pieces inside you, the Kitten elucidated.

The Spy was in a bit of a muddle. She had heard about all-hearing and all-seeing love that just brings people together and helps them to recognize each other even among millions of other people, or to find the loved one even on the moon and bring them back. But this chip was something very rational, and as the Kitten regarded it as something to be utterly taken for granted, the Spy wondered if it wouldn't be better to become a rational person instead.

I'm going to become a rational person, she said, changing the subject. *I won't let myself be so easily influenced by feelings. I'm going to be very rational, almost like a tank.*

The Kitten turned and looked at the Spy with such a startled expression that she was on the verge of laughing. But it was the Kitten who started laughing instead. *Ah, a tank, you say! And where's the barrel to shoot from?* he asked.

What cloud ballerinas men always are! thought the Spy. Her breathing had suddenly become easier and she didn't really want to flee anymore. Life with the Kitten no longer felt so distressing. They both laughed and the Spy felt how the Kitten's chip found it's place in her heart and there turned into thousands of tiny little particles she would never be able to find again.

Black Market-Town-River and the Seven-Headed Man

"Let me, let me, let me show what kind of Man I am..." sang Seven-Headed Man as he came from the eighth of his women. He came through a snowstorm and sang. Nobody was listening. Who was he supposed to show? Only Black Market-Town-River burbled quietly under cover of ice as he passed.

"Let me, let me, let me show what kind of Man I am..." bellowed Seven-Headed Man from his seven throats and sat down in the snow on the rotting bridge.

"Show me, show me," burbled Black Market-Town-River, "show me, show me!"

But Seven-Headed Man started whingeing and all of his seven mouths confided all at the same time in seven languages, for he was also a very intelligent man – "Women are all whores... All my women have been bloody whores, even the loveliest and dearest among them. They've all deceived me in spite of the fact that night and day my fourteen eyes and fourteen ears have tracked them. But I still haven't managed to catch a single gnarled runt of an old man in my women's arms to cut them down to size with my axe." Seven-Headed Man wept. "What, oh what have my innocent eyes had to behold…! Hardly was I out of the house when the gnarled runts of old men arrived on the scene and were straightaway at my women. A young woman is a wanton, very wanton being… I've lived through all of this myself!"

"Hardly, hardly," burbled Black Market-Town-River.

"I've collected material evidence. The amygdalae at the centre of all my seven brains have been working night and day. With tweezers I have collected material evidence from corners and all sorts of recesses, material evidence of deceit. At this very moment I have in my bag hairs from the heads of all my eight women, hairs I have found while investigating the rooms of those gnarled runts of old men. Can there be any more definite material evidence that I've been deceived? Yet more definite material evidence…! And, in addition, their letters and underwear, which I've gathered up round the village!"

"Show me, show me!" burbled Black Market-Town-River.

And Seven-Headed Man brought to light eight hairs, yellowing letters, and rags in several colours. "These are Kati's, these light ones are Marika's, this black one is Nastja's, this one here is Siiri's, these are… Not a one," he sobbed, "not a single one of them has been as monogamous as me!"

Black Market-Town-River laughed. "You certainly are a noteworthy man. But why have you got eight of those women?"

"Why, why! They're women after all and therefore limited beings. And I'm the kind of man who needs to have something to talk about with a woman. Their eight heads and my seven make a proper couple."

Suddenly voices could be heard in the distance. A swarm of madhouse doctors ran towards Seven-Headed Man. From the other side came his eight pregnant women. And directly behind him the mothers of his eight women had crept up with rusty knives in their hands. Seven-Headed Man tried to escape but his trousers had frozen fast to the rotting bridge. He squirmed out of his trousers. The mothers got hold of the little man and cut him down to size. The madhouse doctors poured a jarful of anti-depressants into all of his gobs and his women rolled him off the bridge down into the river.

"Let me show..." bellowed the Man's seven heads in seven languages, and two hands lifted up towards the sky, as if waving farewell, the evidence of his women's guilt – hair, letters, underwear – which he had gone to so much trouble to collect.

Black Market-Town-River carried the freezing Seven-Headed Man downstream, far downstream. "Let me, let me, let me show what kind of River I am!" sang the River.

Evening Rendezvous

"In and of itself I am quite religious," said Happiness Formula, grabbed hold of a pine branch with two fingers, pulled the branch off, stuck it between his lips and looked down at Life Story with a smug look.

Life Story lay on her side in front of him in the soft grass and when Happiness Formula leaned his back against the trunk of the pine tree and stretched a little she saw a bright lilac strip of sky above the sea beyond, a bluish pier and the burning-red noddles of a couple of sea-buoys.

"I'm quite religious," he repeated, "but that doesn't mean that my behaviour is always seemly. I must admit that I'm actually a great ninny."

Life Story gave a start. "I'd like to know why you invited me here today."

Happiness Formula laughed. He looked at Life Story and said slowly, "I suppose to have a bit of fun with you." He grabbed hold of Life Story's slender ankle, lifted the sole of her foot to his mouth and tickled it with the pine branch.

Life Story pulled her foot away. "Aren't you straightforward. But so be it. Doesn't particularly interest me." Life Story turned her back to him and continued to admire the lilac strip of sky, the pier and the fire-red sea buoys. Something rustled at the top of the tree. A strange chattering and grinding could be heard.

Happiness Formula fell silent and looked covetously at Life Story's graceful back.

"You entice everyone. Everyone," said Life Story. "Life Stories bend according to you, turn and twist. You spoil them a little and then leave them behind. And we end our Stories – disappointed, confused, unhappy and without a single formula. Without a single blasted formula!" She felt Happiness Formula's hot breath on the nape of her neck. It intoxicated her. Happiness Formula put his hand on Life Story's neck. "A gnat's bitten you!" He poked Life Story's cheek with the pine branch. "And it's still biting you..." he whispered.

Life Story turned round and looked angrily into Happiness Formula's wantonly flashing eyes. "I'm not a woman. And you're not a man. And even if we were, you know very well how dangerous it is to expect happiness from someone else. You can't even expect happiness from yourself. A Life Story has to concentrate on something else, certainly not on happiness and certainly not on a formula. Then maybe... But don't come enticing me with scented envelopes, thermal socks, favourite ice cream and your There's-A-Remedy-For-Every-Pain philosophy."

"There's a lot more to me than favourite ice cream and thermal socks," Happiness Formula said.

"Right. But I'm happier without you."

And Life Story went away. And down from the pine tree onto her shoulder jumped her Brain's Monkey. And from somewhere high up her Love's Red Pheasant landed on her other shoulder. And she went to look after the garden where her Monkey and Pheasant liked to be. And one evening, when her Monkey was already sleeping, Happiness Formula came like a spring rain. They met unexpectedly on the bluish pier and, by the lustre of the Red Pheasant's feathers and the red sea-buoys, Life Story peeled the Formula off Happiness and Happiness carefully released Life from her Story. They remained as Happiness and Life, who became part of one another on that darkening pier. Not a single word, or gnat, or pine branch.

Stone Chunk and Beautiful Question

"WHO AM I?" Stone Chunk asked himself. "Who am I to judge others?"

But the judgement had already been made. Stone Chunk had only one more question as gossamer as air, but even that soon vanished. A conviction took shape within him that was as firm as stone – "Beautiful Question, the partner of my life, really isn't a Beautiful Question, but only a chunk of flesh."

Stone Chunk flinched. "And what is that chunk of flesh doing now?" he wanted to know.

And the answer that Stone Chunk gave himself was by no means beautiful – "Beautiful Question, who veils herself behind that beautiful name, is giving herself to pleasures of the flesh. For she is, after all, flesh like me. And what else should flesh do but find ceaseless shameless pleasure in itself?"

Beautiful Question came into the room and didn't know that Stone Chunk had in the meantime come up with an answer. Unsuspectingly she did what came into her head and laughed, for she was cheerful and even a bit frolicsome. She flitted about and sang. Stone Chunk didn't like this at all. He had been taught that where there is flitting about and singing you should look for the basest deceit.

"Beautiful Question," said Stone Chunk, "you're interesting."

Beautiful Question gave a start and swept her straight northland Finno-Ugric hair in a great ark over her head. But her hair didn't fall down again. It remained standing straight up on her head. "Hair, hair, fall down now, won't you?" Beautiful Question pleaded, laughing. But her hair stayed standing up on end as if something had frightened it from the root to the tip of every strand.

Beautiful Question smiled and decided to take what she had just heard as a compliment, although she wasn't really sure. "That's grand," she thought, "that I'm so interesting to him, But I wonder why my hair took such terrible fright?"

"Yes, interesting that it's so interesting…" Stone Chunk procrastinated and looked at Beautiful Question with his only angry answering eye. Beautiful Question smiled again, but her heart skipped a few beats. "Heart-heart, what's this all about!" Beautiful Question protested. But her heart continued in some strange self-determined rhythm. Beautiful Question kindly offered Stone Chunk a cup of tea.

When Stone Chunk told Beautiful Question for the third time that she was interesting, her blood began to curdle at the sound of his voice. "Blood-blood, why have you started to curdle like this?" she asked to herself.

"Stupid Question," grunted Blood. "That Stone Chunk has secretly come up with an answer to you. And a very wrong answer."

"Well, what a very interesting story," thought Beautiful Question. "Hair and Heart and Blood fear that I've been answered wrongly. But this Stone Chunk here said nothing more than that I'm interesting. Interesting, what could he have meant by that?"

Winter came, the sea froze over and boats didn't sail anymore between the rest of the world and Stone Chunk's and Beautiful Question's home. And one evening Stone Chunk told Beautiful Question right to her face, "You're really not Beautiful Question, you're a Piece of Flesh." Beautiful Question's smile was smothered. "That is the answer then that Hair and Heart and Blood warned me about!"

"And you're not Stone Chunk," she screamed angrily, "You're, you're... Wrong Answer!"

And so Beautiful Question, who to Stone Chunk's mind was a Piece of Flesh, and Stone Chunk, who to Beautiful Question's mind was Wrong Answer, lived together for some time.

And Beautiful Question's Hair began to go grey with horror and Blood to flow more carefully and Heart often did that rhythm trick. And Beauty began to gradually peel off from Question, for the Wrong in Answer flayed her and scraped her – rawly and lusting for flesh.

But a Question remained. That Question was, "Why, on that beautiful evening, was I answered so wrongly?" And Beautiful Question continued to repeat that not at all beautiful question to herself for a long time, hoping that somewhere within her an answer would be born.

But the answer wasn't born. Not yet. Instead Stone Chunk swaggered day after day with his wrong answer. And as soon as Beautiful Question was herself again – beautiful all over and question all over, Stone Chunk came out with his wrong answer. He boasted again and again, "I love truth and I love daring. And even if the truth isn't beautiful, I dare to say it out loud. You are Piece of Flesh, who veils herself behind that beautiful question, Flesh who gave herself that evening to pleasures of the flesh, for what else could Flesh do without me, other than to feel joy unceasingly and shamelessly. I dare say I know, for I'm Stone Chunk and I know how to be objective even if there's no profit in it for me." So swaggered Stone Chunk. And he also said, "My whole life is dedicated to the truth."

For Beautiful Question this truth was nothing other than a base and cruel accusation. She ran out of the room. It was an oh-so-moonlit night! Water sparkled serenely in the sea and it was so quiet that Beautiful Question's every breath could be heard a long way off. Beautiful Question tried to dance a little, for to her mind this silence was the most beautiful music. And she did dance and before long found herself in an altogether different kind of time and space. And very soon an Answer began to ripen within her. An Answer that was only one of many, but certainly not wrong.

River of Song

I

In a barge that had gone under long-long ago and sunk deep down to the bottom of the River of Song, ten red milky-whiskered kittens had made their nest. Their youngest brother, a small water-grey cat who hadn't even opened his eyes yet, lived there too.

Like all of them, he had been born on dry land under the steps of an old timber house. When he had found his feet, he tottered into the yard together with his brothers and sisters into the light of day. Falling over again and again he crept into the shade under the rhubarb, for something of unprecedented glare and glitter had forced its way in behind his still-closed eyelids. Uh-oh… He fell asleep with his head on his paws, without knowing that this would be his last sleep above the surface of the river.

The owner gathered all the tottering kittens together, even the grey one dozing pleasantly under the rhubarb leaf.

He gathered all the kittens into a rag, put a rough stone into the middle to weigh it down, and tied the bundle together tightly. For the time being his wife had taken the kittens' caterwauling, clawing mother into the shed. *Splash*… the man threw the wriggling bundle of cats into the surge of the River of Song. Silently, swiftly the struggling nest sank to the bottom.

Oh, how bad it is underwater, the kittens thought. *Oh, how bad*… They whimpered and tried to call their mother, but nothing helped. From between the bulrushes came Death, a scythe of cyperus in his hand, who undid the bundle and gave them a fresh underwater breath of life. The little cats came to and teetered on along the muddy river bottom and slippery stones.

Creak, Death with his scythe of cyperus pushed open the door of the barge and counted up ten red kittens. *There seemed to be another one… ah, there he comes.* The grey kitten's tail had become caught in a battered doll's pram that had once slipped out of the hands of a little girl and rolled down the bank into the River of Song. Now it clattered along attached to the tail of the kitten, like a big cart. Death with his scythe of cyperus unloosed the pram, picked the kitten up in the palm of his hand, and put it in through the door of the barge. *Creak*, he closed the door.

In the galley the grey kitten chose as his nest an open first aid cupboard which was tilted over to one side. There he now slept purring away, his head on a bandage roll and his hind legs stretched over an empty bottle of iodine.

Thread tails, button eyes, milk whiskers, marzipan noses, brush paws, sleep well, he heard his mother's voice saying through his dreams.

Creak, the barge door went again, when the kittens tottered out in the morning. They were already a bit bigger. Like the buds of blossoms they had swelled in the night, and all but the grey kitten had opened their eyes. Death with his scythe of cyperus had led a blue sea cow to the place and milked bright white milk into a big clay bowl. All of the underwater cats gratefully set about lapping up the milk. Only the grey kitten didn't immediately find a space at the edge of the bowl and instead asked the cow, *How long have you been living here underwater?*

Moons, many moons, the cow answered, and looked at him kindly. The rusty doll's pram swayed in the current, the kitten turned round and with his paw touched the white orris roots that ran like the strings of an instrument over the pram. *Plink, plink, tinkle, tinkle...* went the roots and all the underwater dwellers stopped to listen.

Moons, moons, the cow repeated again and nodded pensively.

The grey kitten played and played with the strings of orris root and the doll 's pram chimed under his paws. Death put his scythe of cyperus on a stone and closed his eyes. *Oh,* he thought, *what a find!*

II

In the meantime there was silence and the willow catkins dropped high above their heads into their own dark shadows on the surface of the river. The wind played with the bulrush seeds along the riverside, and an aspen dugout canoe, in which two maidens and a young man were sitting, ploughed silently up along the crest of the river. One of the maidens sang and the other was silent, and almost without a sound the paddles caught their own dark reflections in the depths of the water. The one girl's voice was as clear as a silver paddle and the other's silence was even more beautiful, and the young man didn't know which one the roots of his heart's tree were more entwined with. They were People of the Meadow. All at once they lowered their heads so as not to break the fragile spiderweb that had been cast over the river. They slipped through under the spiderweb and straightened their backs again.

Tatõn mur, the young man said in the language of the People of the Meadow. That meant it's deep here. The girls nodded, knowing that the depths had taken a fair few from among their midst.

Now the aspen canoe slipped over a big splash of sunlight and the People of the Meadow saw how a maiden of the Ovda folk who had been sitting on a fallen tree branch washing her backwards feet threw her breasts over her shoulders with a start and, pulling her brown hair down to cover her nakedness, plunged into the forest. That maiden, who was called Tsheber Ovda, grasped the mane of a horse stolen from the village of the People of the Meadow, heaved herself onto the stallion's back and dug her backwards soles into the steed's groin. He sped over the field yellow with globeflowers, buttercups and marigolds, and the cuckoos and starlings fled out of his way bumping into each other in alarm. *To my own kind, back to my own kind,* Tsheber Ovda mumbled to herself.

Slurping the milk of the blue cow, the grey kitten opened his eyes. Like gates they opened up for the first time to the underwater world – to the barge and the little reflected flame next to it that had kindled itself as it often did when the sunlight played on the surface of the river.

Look, it's as if there's a flame burning down there, the young man whispered and he poked the paddle into the glowing heart of the flashing splash of sunlight. And the maiden who hadn't been silent sang, *Like a flame burning there, like a flame burning down there...* She looked the young man straight in the eye and laughed. And the maiden who was silent suffered the blinding light, looked through the brightening water and really saw how ten rowan red kittens warmed themselves around the underwater flame. But the light grey kitten dozed in the clay milk bowl which he had first licked so clean that there wasn't a drop left.

But the young man thought about Tsheber Ovda, how

she had hidden her body white as day under her hair, how the ball of her foot touched the ground before her heel when she ran, how her breasts waved behind her like banners when she rode away, how she feared him, a Man of the Meadow, how she had clawed and bitten when the young man had once caught her in the sunlight of the riverbank, how he had roughly torn the beads from the neck of the Ovda maiden, clumsily embraced her and cast off the belt from around her waist, wrenched the rings from her fingers, and thrown all these riches into the blackening River of Song. The maiden went limp, benumbed in his hands, the hot tears flowing down her body like rapids. *They're not paid for yet, don't you understand, I still have to pay for them, pay a high price for them...* the maiden cried. The young man wanted to console her and said, *I'll buy you new ones, presents from me, even more expensive, don't cry lovely Ovda.* But the maiden, wet with tears, slipped out of his hands and fled into the forest. Until that day the young man remembered Tsheber Ovda's pitiless weeping that had cut the meadow of his soul like a scythe. What did Tsheber Ovda mean when she complained that she still had to pay for the things he had thrown into the River of Song? All the People of the Meadow knew that Ovdas are eternal thieves. Perhaps this girl's valuables were from the dowry chest of some Girl of the Meadow that the Ovdas had prised open and emptied by the light of the moon.

Now, as the young man paddled along in a dugout canoe with two young beauties he had met the very same Ovda again.

Three weddings are given to a Person of the Meadow, sang the maiden in the dugout canoe who wasn't silent. *First of all the wedding with life.* The maiden's voice shimmered like the river. *Then the wedding with another Person of the Meadow. ANOTHER PERSON OF THE MEADOW,* she repeated, and again gave the young Man of the Meadow a penetrating look. *And finally...* she looked down and her voice ploughed the River of Song deeply and quietly, ... *the wedding with death. This is the backwards wedding, THE BACKWARDS WEDDING...*

Backwards like my reflections in the River of Song, backwards like the soles of the Ovda's feet, mused the young Man of the Meadow.

III

That time he hadn't dared to follow Tsheber Ovdas's tracks to catch her. And so there was no more rest to be had for him, day or night. In the end he went away to the town, where the river was said to flow with gold and the land to grow crisp-baked bread. But he fell ill like all People of the Meadow there. *Meadow longings,* was the doctor's diagnosis. A treatment was prescribed: a precise dose of bird-cherry scent directly into the lungs, drops of wide open space directly into the eyeballs, tablets of the glow of sunset, baths of earth for his hands and small electric shocks for his feet from a stinging nettle device to enliven him a little out of the listlessness that had filled the whole of the young man's soul. The People of the Meadow beside him in the ward died one after the other, but first their tongues were deadened to stop them from lamenting and calling out and infecting healthy town people with meadow longings. *Earth cracks, even stone breaks, but People of the Meadow have to endure...* the young man repeated his grandfather's saying to himself. But he didn't hold out. He suddenly fled in the month of the summer solstice, when the sphere of the heavens had risen as high as high can be. Fled from the others as well as himself before stepping onto the stinging nettle device. Fled barefoot, slipping like a summer wind towards the horizon, surrendering to meadow longings more and more with each new step.

But in his home village on the banks of the winding River of Song between the meadows the stream of life had begun to dry up. Nearly everyone of his age had had their tongues deadened in the towns, and their children were born outright tongueless. Old toothless men and women told tales of bygone days and so tried to still the pain of their loss. Then he found these two maidens in his home village. The one who wasn't silent ploughed the River of Song with the silver paddle of her voice. And the one who was silent was silent in the language of the People of the Meadow, so that everything in her silence was clear, pure and beautiful. Has she still got a tongue? The young man didn't know.

At the edge of the forest Tsheber Ovda jumped down from her horse and hopped along the marsh mattocks to the lush marsh island amid the misty bog. The horse whinnied fearfully when the Ovda maiden left him alone tied to a tree. Although she didn't remember, she had already lost some ten horses in this way, horses that had been stolen with a great deal of trouble. In the night wolves had come and torn apart the horses that had been tied up snorting in fear for their lives. The wolves had ripped the flesh from their bones, dragged the carcasses high up onto the riverbank and howled to the moon as if they were singing the horses' funeral song. There the skeletons now lay – bleached, lightning white, a warning to all horses who fall victim to the Ovdas' passion for riding and to their heedlessness.

The dugout canoe of the People of the Meadow with the young man and the two maidens glided past these very same lightning-white skeletons. They looked silently at the horse carcasses high up on the riverbank and even the maiden who wasn't silent closed her singing mouth for a moment. They paddled the canoe into a quiet current, stepped onto the shore and gazed with dismay at the devastation that had been worked by the wolves. The horses' skeletons rattled in the summer breeze, and partridges had made nests between the bones.

Suddenly the young man took to his heels – back upstream after the fleeing Tsheber Ovda. Out of breath he reached the edge of the marsh and found the Ovda maiden's horse. He untied him from the tree and the black stallion whinnied in gratitude. Swiftly he led the horse back along the way he had come to the horses' cemetery where the two Maidens of the Meadow were waiting between the partridge nests.

The River of Song murmured its unceasing song over stones and tree roots, over all the shy beings within it, murmured over mysteries precious as anything can be, over the pieces of jewellery made especially beautiful by their loss. And the doll's pram with strings of orris root chimed from the bottom of the river, *plink, tinkle, plink, tinkle...*

Along with the black stallion the young Man of the Meadow had rescued his own heart from the fetters of the Ovda maiden. But how they went on – whether along still waters or racing headlong on the back of the stallion, where they came to and what they found before them – only the meadow wind knows.

Lightning Source UK Ltd.
Milton Keynes UK
25 September 2009

144153UK00001B/3/P

9 780906 672921